For Maisie
Lucy ♥ and
Jackie
McKimmie.

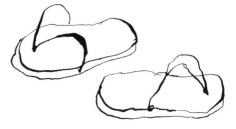

Maisie Moo and Invisible Lucy

Chris McKimmie

ALLEN&UNWIN

My name is **Maisie Moo**.
I live in a palace in the
middle of nowhere.
The **Gone Bonkers Discount Palace**.
We sell all sorts of stuff.
Mainly gondolas.

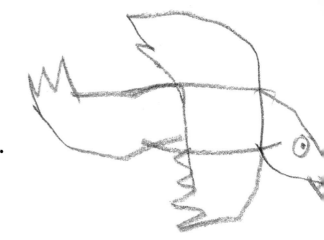

'It's a silly name for a shop,' says **Invisible lucy**.

**My favourite
colour is magenta
polka dots.**

My best friend is Invisible Lucy.

Every morning, as sure as sunshine,
Drongo wakes me up.
This is a Drongo day:
a walk,
breakfast,
more sleeps.

He is as lazy as a pillow.
His favourite letter is
ZZZZzzzzzzz...
Dad bought Drongo to
guard us.

'Neville! It's that dog again!'

Mum says Drongo would help a burglar pack the sack if we had stuff worth stealing.

On his walks he growls
at the garden
gnomes.
They don't
hiss,
shout
or
growl
back.
He is a bit
of a
scaredy cat.
*'He is a bit
of a dill,'*
says Invisible
lucy.

This is what I like:
my dog Drongo,
sleeping in,
playing
the drums.

Invisible lucy likes
what I like.

Her favourite letter is
M for Maisie Moo.

m

Dad calls me
  his little angel.
I don't want
  to be an angel.

I am **always** the angel in
  the **V**enice **C**hristmas concert.
I would rather play the **drums**
  or
      be the **donkey.**
        'Not the bum bit,'
          says Invisible **l**ucy.

Christmas is coming again.
The tourists are in town.
I have to help Mum
in the shop.
Dad will be home soon.

Dad drives a truck.

He isn't home much.

When he is home
he tells me stories and
does sound effects.
like this:

iT was a dark
and stormy
night
WOOOOOOO

I was sound asleep
in the truck at
Mooball ZZZZZZ
Thunder rolled
across the sky
like a thousand
drums BOOM
BOOM
BOOM
BOOM

then i
was
falling
down
down
down

HA HA HA

'Goodnight, little angel.'

Six sleeps to
Christmas.

I slept in.

'Uh oh,'
said Invisible Lucy.

I was supposed
to be helping
Mum.

'We don't want to sweep!'

hissed Invisible Lucy.

VENICE

S VENICE   P VENICE

Venice

venice

I don't
WA
Swee
junk
shop!

4 POSTCARDS
5 Plastic flowers
6 Novelty glasses
7 Hats / pins / caps
8
9 Gondolas
10 ruffles
11 Koala Bear clocks
12 Velvet cushions
13 T Thongs
14 Posters
15
16 key rings
17 Salt spoons
18 Magnet
19 Pencils
20 mugs
21 Bags

Invisible lucy
kicked
a box of
gondolas.

They
scattered
like stars.

'Maisie!'
'It wasn't me,
it was lucy!'
Mum went nuts.
'OK...Lucy
can leave
NOW!'
She opened
the door.

'OUT!'

I spent the
rest of the
day upstairs
in my room.
I didn't want to
talk to anyone.

Not Mum.
Not Dad.
Not Drongo.

I played the
drums a bit and
went to bed
early.

' Sweet dreams,
   Maisie
     Moonbeam.'

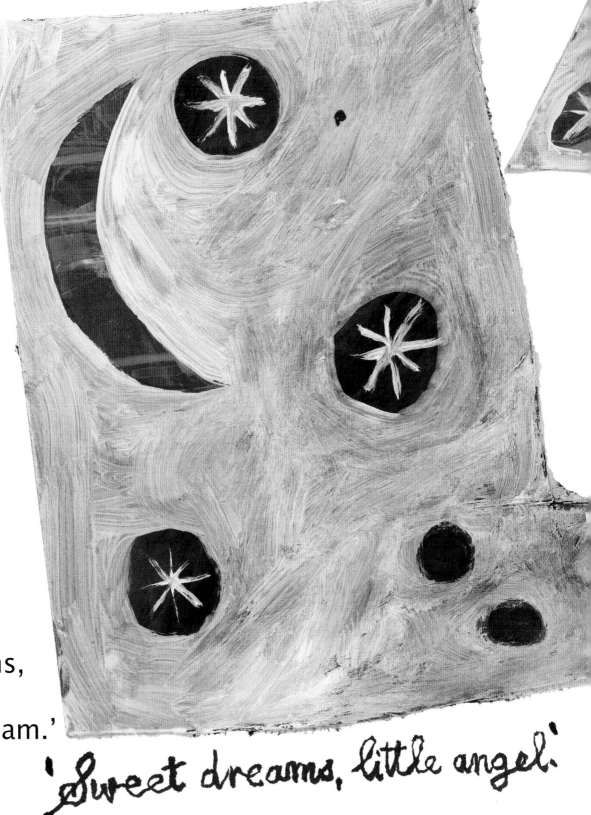

'Sweet dreams, little angel.'

The next morning
    I slept in again.

The earth was
  as red as
toffee apples
  and the
    clouds
  as pink as
      fairy floss
        from the
          Royal Show.

Bacon and eggs were cooking
And toast.
Two kookaburras were
laughing in the kitchen.

Dad was home.

At the Venice
Christmas concert,
I wasn't
the angel.
I wasn't
the donkey.
But I got to play
'Silent Night' on my
drums.

'Love it,'
said Invisible Lucy.

Mum and Dad
loved it too.

It was all a little bit wonderful.

First published in 2007

Copyright © Chris McKimmie, 2007
text and illustrations,

Thanks
to my sister
Sandra and my
sister-in-law
Robin for advice

on invisible people.

The author and publisher
wish to thank
Pim Mulder and Peter Rofe
of the real
Gone Bonkers Discount Chain
in Queensland for the
use of their name.

Allen & Unwin
83 Alexander St
Crows Nest NSW 2065
Australia
Phone: (61 2) 8425 0100
Fax: (61 2) 9906 2218
Email: info@allenandunwin.com
Web: www.allenandunwin.com

National Library of Australia
Cataloguing-in-Publication entry:
McKimmie, Chris.
Maisie Moo and Invisible Lucy.
For children.
ISBN 9781741751345
1. Father and child-Australia-Juvenile fiction. I. Title.
A823.3

Book design, font design and lettering by
Chris McKimmie
Set in
dylanandblake
Printed in China by
Everbest Printing Co

10 9 8 7 6 5 4 3 2 1

The pictures
are done with acrylic paint on mdf board,
canvas and paper.
Some pictures are painted with
watercolour and some drawn with
ink and pencil.